For everyone who listens,
for everyone who needs
to be listened to.
J.C.

For the three girls I love to listen to.
R.W.

EGMONT

We bring stories to life

First published in 2019 by Egmont UK Limited
The Yellow Building, 1 Nicholas Road, London W11 4AN

www.egmont.co.uk

Text copyright © Joseph Coelho 2019
Illustrations copyright © Robyn Wilson-Owen 2019

Joseph Coelho and Robyn Wilson-Owen have asserted their moral rights.

ISBN 978 1 4052 9129 3

A CIP catalogue record for this title is available from the British Library.

Stay safe online. Egmont is not responsible for content hosted by third parties.

Egmont takes its responsibility to the planet and its inhabitants very seriously.
We aim to use papers from well-managed forests run by responsible suppliers.

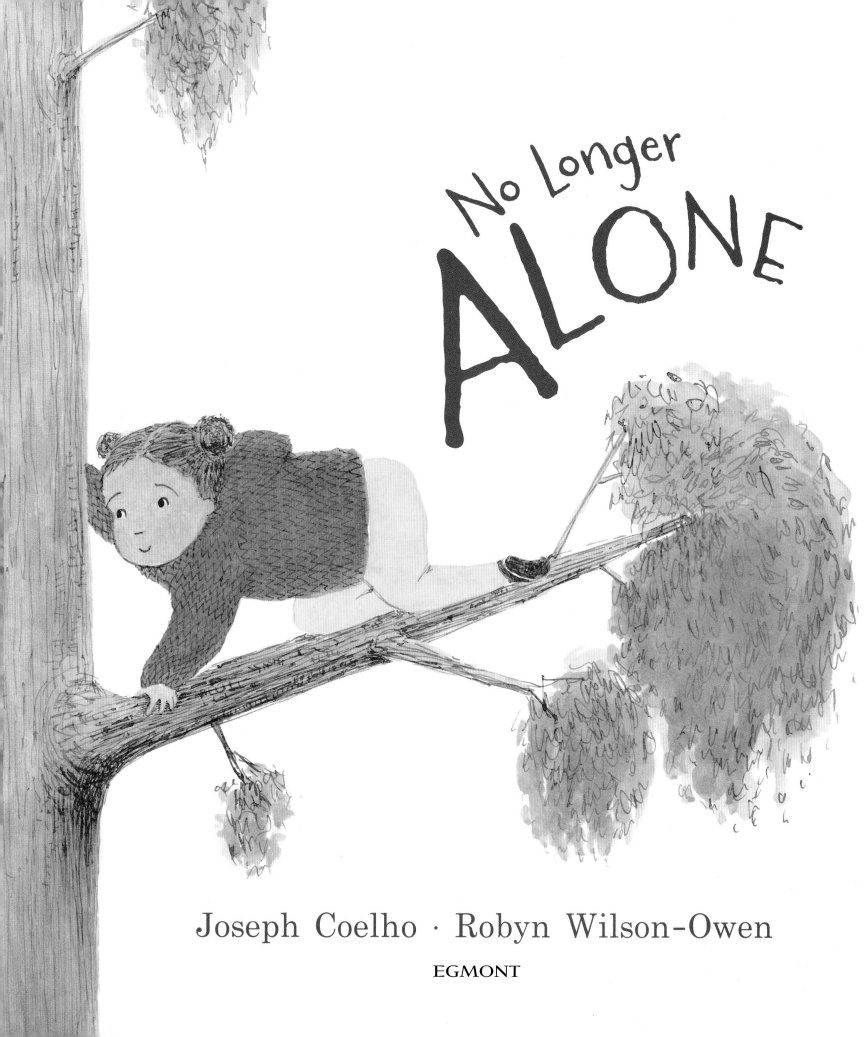

No Longer ALONE

Joseph Coelho · Robyn Wilson-Owen

EGMONT

Aunty says . . . "She's shy."
Whenever we bump into people in the street.

But I'm not shy,
I just don't feel like
talking right now.

And when I do feel like talking
I can talk non-stop!
Like I do when I'm alone . . .

I talk the leaves off the trees.
I talk the birds out of the sky.

I talk the stars out of the Milky Way.

I talk of darkness and tears, of loneliness and fears.

I talk and talk, and I'm **not shy**.

My teacher says . . . "She's very quiet."
Whenever I'm working in a group.

But I'm not quiet, I just don't
feel like making a noise right now.

And when I do feel like making a noise . . .

I make a racket!
Like I do when
I'm alone . . .

I sing the depths of whale song.

I summon the ocean's roar.

I orchestrate the stampede of sea storms.

I collect sobs and stopper-up wails.

I shout and I scream,
and I am **not quiet**!

Nan says . . . "She doesn't like
to run about." Whenever we're
at the park with my sisters.

But I just don't feel like running about
with my sisters right now.

And when I do feel like running about,
I run riot.

Like I do when I'm alone . . .

I swing over chasms, stumble through swamps,
balance between ice-capped mountains,
climb up old rotten trees . . .

. . . hide under the stairs,
kneel in the gloom,
stare with blurry eyes.

Dad says . . . . "Try to be the old you, the get-up-and-go you. The loud-and-active you, the happy you, the you, you used to be."

And I tell him that
that was the old me,
the before me, the
once-upon-a-time me,
the before-I-was-sad me,
before we were alone.

I tell him how I don't
feel myself right now,
how I feel different,
like someone else.
I tell him all the things
that are worrying me,
upsetting me, making
me feel alone.

And he listens . . . like the sun listens to leaves,
like the ocean listens to raindrops,
like the stars listen to the glide of their planets.

And right **now** starts to feel different.

Aunty says . . . "Oh she loves talking."

Whenever we bump into people in the
street and I ask them a ton of questions.

But I don't love talking,
I just feel more like talking now,
like I did when I was alone.

My teacher says . . . "She's very loud."
When I'm telling everyone in my group what to do.

But I'm not very loud,
I just feel more like being loud now,
like I did when I was alone.

Nan says . . . "She'll run circles
around you two." Whenever I'm
in the park with my sisters.

But I don't run circles around them . . .
I run with them, and play with them,
and we swing over the birds in the sky,

and we play and we talk
and we share what we feel,
what we see and what we imagine.

And we no longer
feel alone.